ISBN 978-099625254-6

Design:
David Robson, Robson Design

Published by
AMPERSAND, INC.
1050 North State Street
Chicago, Illinois 60610
—
203 Finland Place
New Orleans, Louisiana 70131

www.ampersandworks.com

Produced and Published in the United States
Printed in U.S.A.
1st Edition

To request a personalized copy or to schedule
a book signing/school reading, email
nancyegee@sbcglobal.net

a nancy gee book

The SECRET PATH

Written by Nancy Gee • Illustrated by Kathleen Newman

AMP&RSAND, INC.

Chicago • New Orleans

STUDENT REVIEWS
from Willow Elementary School in Homewood, Illinois

"This book is good for young readers because it introduces rhyming words. And then you learn a lesson at the end of the story. You have to stick together."
Benjamin

"I like that it tells a true story and it rhymes."
Caylum

"I like how it has a bunch of new creatures compared to the first book, *The Secret Drawer*."
Declan

"I loved the pictures! The words rhyme. I love rhyming! It looked like fiction but it is non-fiction. I love the book!"
Quinn

"I thought the story was entertaining. It had a lot of action."
Anika

"I thought it was a great book because it taught people and friends how to help each other."
Macy

"I loved the way she made the pictures come to life! I just feel it happening to me! I felt like I was right there in the story. She really did a good job."
Kate

"Unpredictable, family friendly, rhyming, adventurous book."
Sumayyah and Grace

The Secret Path is dedicated to
my grandboys, Grey and Blain, for inspiring me
to write this story, and to all the children
who have come to love my first book, *The Secret Drawer.*
Their interest in flying squirrels
has encouraged me to keep on writing!
Nancy Gee

Al, do you remember last year,
Trapped in the Secret Drawer in fear?

Let's make the journey back
With our friends, as a pack.

We'll bring news for all to share.
Maddie and Kitty will surely care.

Let's start running really fast.
We must hurry to complete our task.

Sal, let's take the path we know so well.
But, Al, this path is quicker, I can tell.

Slow down, Sal! You're much too fast!
We must rest or we'll not last.

Oh my, Sal! You've run out of sight!
You're giving us all a terrible fright.

From a distance your cries we hear.
And you're in trouble, we do fear.

Hurry, hurry! Over here!
Keep on coming, you must be near!

Down this hole I'm sure Sal fell.
But where she is I cannot tell.

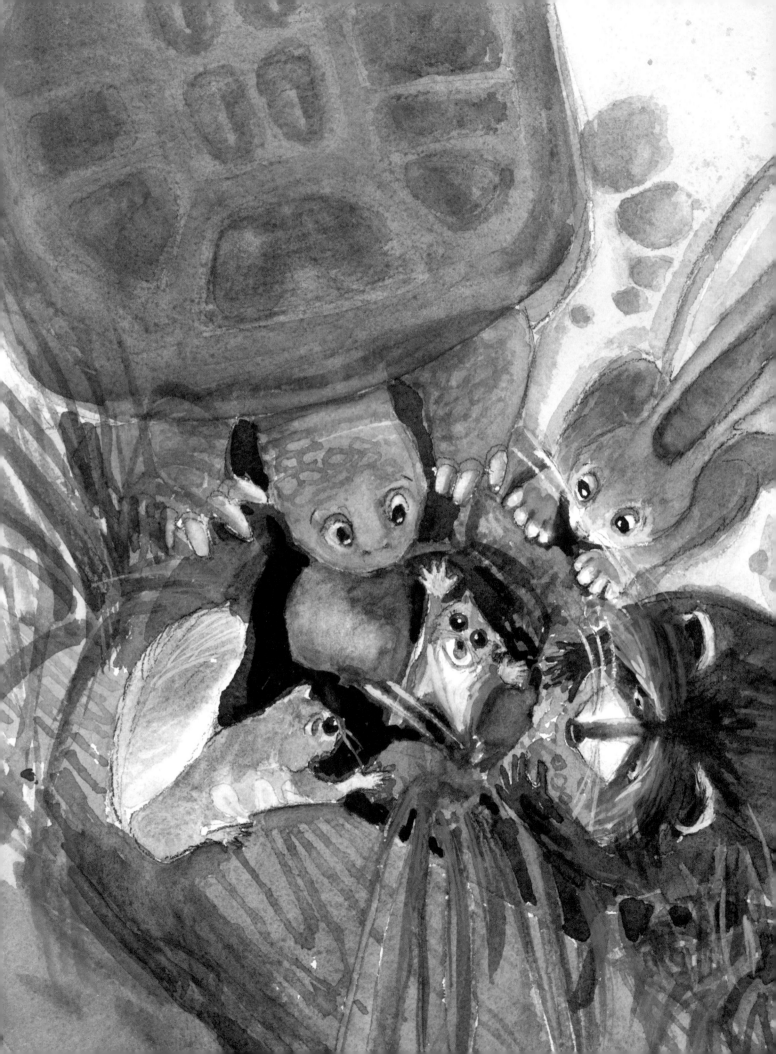

Al, I'm stuck down here and all alone.
My foot is trapped beneath a stone.

It's cold and damp, the water's coming down!
Please rescue me before I drown!

Turtle's too wide and will not fit.

Raccoon's too round and will only stick.

Bunny's ears are much too tall.

And, Al, it's far for you to fall!

Thunder, lightning fill the sky.
Pouring rain could make me cry!

Go find Kitty, he'll fix my plight.
We need him *now* to make it right.

No time to lose, you must scat.
And find our friend, the Kitty cat.

Kitty! Kitty! Look who's here!
Al and friends from far and near.

But something's wrong. Where is Sal?
Al would never leave his pal.

Oh! They're going back from where they came.
Through thunder, lightning and pouring rain.

Al keeps looking for us to follow.
He is running toward that hollow.

Turtle's covering that hole to protect
Sal, who's down there, I suspect.

Sal, Kitty is here
to play his role.

He'll save you from
this dark, wet hole.

Kitty pushes and pulls
with all his might

Moving that stone
to make Sal right.

Sal's foot's been hurt and needs some care.
But we must travel. There's news to share.

Rest now, Sal. Ride on Raccoon's back.
We'll keep together and stay on track.

The news is coming and coming fast!
Maddie's slipper is Sal's at last!

Kitty finds a sock, we know not where.
He wraps Sal's foot with tender, loving care.

Sleep Sal, sleep, safe now from your fall.
Time to rest and wait for Sal to call.

The news is here! The news is there!
The news is humming everywhere!!!

Baby Als and Sals so fair!
Home they came with news to share
With special friends who truly care.

BABY FLYING SQUIRREL FACTS

How many babies does one mother count?
Two to seven is the average amount.

What time of year are babies born?
Spring and summer because it's warm.

When they're born, why are eyes closed tight?
Their first month is dark, then eyes open to the night.

When they're born, can they hear?
Six days later, ears appear.

Why are their tails like pencils, rounded and tight?
It takes a month for them to flatten for flight.

Why are they born with only one toe?
In just one week, four will grow.

After two months, they start to fly.
Flat tails and flaps let them glide through the sky.
As long as mom is with them, they go everywhere.
Gliding here and there, almost anywhere!

NANCY GEE, Author, expresses her love of nature while stirring the imaginations and hearts of children of all ages. This is her second picture book, a sequel to the first, *The Secret Drawer*, winner of the coveted Gold Award from Mom's Choice. Nancy lives in Orland Park, Illinois with her husband. She is Owner and President of Maywood Industries, Inc., a company that manufactures specialty crating and sells building materials throughout the Chicagoland area. Nancy is a graduate of Drake University. **www.anancygeebook.com**

KATHLEEN NEWMAN began coloring with crayons at a very early age and has since won numerous awards for her pastel, oil and watercolor paintings. She teaches painting workshops throughout the United States and weekly classes at the Old Town Art Center in Chicago. She and her husband live in Palos Park, Illinois. Kathleen is thrilled to illustrate her first picture book with Nancy Gee. **www.kathleennewman.com**